To Thomas,

Best Wishes,

Janette Bond

May 2011

The Fair Folk of Doon Hill

Janette Bond

author HOUSE®

AuthorHouse™ UK Ltd.
500 Avebury Boulevard
Central Milton Keynes, MK9 2BE
www.authorhouse.co.uk
Phone: 08001974150

First published by AuthorHouse 3/19/2010

ISBN: 978-1-4490-9911-4 (sc)

This book is printed on acid-free paper.

Introduction

Deep in the heart of the Trossachs countryside, in Scotland, lies the village of Aberfoyle. To the south east of the village is a hill called Doon Hill. Legend has it that this is the home of the Sidhe (pronounced shee), or Faery Folk. It is said that in 1692, the minister of the parish, Reverend Robert Kirk, was spirited away by the Faery Folk as a punishment for revealing their secrets. This novel is based on the legend, paying particular attention to Robert Kirk's own manuscripts.

Meet Hamish, his granny and other characters inside this book. They are gnomes, guardians of the oak trees. Their homeland; the woody knoll called Doon Hill. Their duty; to take care of sick animals and to protect the oak woodlands. Their biggest enemy; owls! Their greatest delight; to sing and dance celebrating the forest gods. Their biggest hate; humans who call them faeries, blame them for troubles and show them no respect.

Chapter 1

Hamish yawned, stretching himself to his full height of twelve inches. Although having slept for many hours he was still tired.
"Hamish! You up yet? Porridge's ready!"

His grandmother's voice filtered from the cooking chamber into his sleeping chamber and stirred his brain into action. Hamish was always hungry! Jumping up from the warm depths of his bed, he splashed water onto his face from the washing bowl in the corner and struggled into his green, woolly work clothes. He allowed his nose to guide him to the cooking chamber where his grandmother had filled his bowl with steaming porridge and was now spooning golden honey on top.

"Top of the morning to you, Hamish," said his grandmother.
"Morning Granny," Hamish answered, looking not at her but at his breakfast. Food first, folk second, that was his motto!
"And which duty are you to be doing today?" she asked.
"Wildlife check, north side area, lots of birds nesting at the moment," he mumbled, through slurps of honey porridge.
"Aye, it's a time when the human folk are always

snooping, stealing eggs. They don't even eat them, you know, just blow out the yolk and keep the egg shell. They're queer, strange beings are humans," Granny replied.

"Sometimes they destroy the nest too, Calum says so," agreed Hamish.

"Where can Calum be this morning? He should be back from the night duty by now. I hope no owl has gotten him," said Granny.

"Nah! He's too fly for that," answered Hamish. "Got to go now Gran, Cheerie Bye!"

With that, Hamish bounced off his seat and made for the door. There was no way he was going to show up for work late. He slammed the door in his haste and made his way up the staircase of tree roots. On reaching the top, he squeezed his head out into the open air and searched the sky for owls. His Granny's warning was always with him. Other than humans, the only enemy the "*Fair Folk*" had, were owls. He had just enjoyed his breakfast; he had no wish to become supper for some sleepy owl coming home to roost. All clear! He scrambled up and ran along the worn path until he reached a much bigger and older oak tree than his own. He crouched down and slipped between the intricate roots, down into a vast chamber underneath the tree. *Fair Folk Head Quarters!*

Hamish and his clan, were actually gnomes,

guardians of the oak trees. Their homeland; a woody knoll in Central Scotland, called Doon Hill. Their duty; to take care of sick animals and to protect the oak woodlands. Their biggest enemy; owls! Their greatest delight; to sing and dance celebrating the forest gods. Their biggest hate; humans who called them faeries, blamed them for troubles and showed them no respect.

On entering the chamber Hamish was immediately swallowed up into the crowd of folk waiting instructions from The Chief. Gradually they all began to turn and face a large, wooden chair situated on a platform, at the far end of the chamber. Its arms were carved with creatures of the woods and the back was carved into the shape of an ancient oak tree in summer. Its legs resembled branches of the oak tree, each resting on a carved acorn. An eerie silence descended and from nowhere appeared a gnome, who seemed not only larger but also much older than the congregation of gnomes looking silently towards the oak throne. He wore a crown of oak leaves and carried a staff of thick oak. Chief Fernlea of Doon Hill was ready to relay his daily instructions to his clan

"Good morning to you all," began Chief Fernlea, sometimes known as Fiery Fernlea because of his bright red hair and a temper to match. "Before we discuss our daily duties I have grave news to tell you. As you know, our food stores are low in early Spring and it is difficult to find food before the new season's crops are ready to be harvested. Last night, part of the night shift had been given the duty of foraging in the barns of Campbell's farm. Some of them were in the hen house taking eggs when they were disturbed by an angry fox. They all had to scatter and make their own way home as best they could. Three members of the patrol have not arrived home. They have not been seen since the fox attacked. They may be injured or at worst perished in the claws of the fox or a passing owl. Whilst doing your duties today you must be extra careful and search your area for them. No patrol can return to Campbell's farm until darkness tonight to look for them. It would not be wise to be seen by the humans. May the Forest Gods take care of you on your journeys today."

Chief Fernlea left as quickly and quietly as he had arrived. Hamish was stunned. Was Calum, his brother, one of the missing? Was Calum dead? How could he tell Granny Calum wasn't going to come home?

Chapter 2

Misty was suddenly aware she was talking to herself. Hamish was not beside her. She turned around. Hamish was still standing in the same place, rooted to the spot like one of the oaks on the hill. Her initial reaction was to yell at him but she stopped herself just in time, as she saw his eyes had a faraway look, as if his mind had moved off to another place. Cautiously she walked back to stand beside him. He did not seem to be aware she was even there.

"Hamish," she said, quietly, "Hamish, we need to go."

He gradually turned his head towards her. His eyes distant and his voice barely a whisper. "Calum is not home."

She understood. Calum was one of the missing night shift!

"We need to go, Hamish. We have work to do and part of that work is to see if we can find Calum."

"You mean he may not be dead. Not savaged by the fox or eaten by an owl?"

"Maybe not. He could be in need of help, our help. We need to go."

"We need to go," he repeated. Then louder, "We need to go!"

They left Head Quarters and made their way through the oak trees to the northern edge of the Hill. Not a word was spoken between them. They followed no path as there were none to follow. The Fair Folk believe that the manufacture of paths only encourages humans to follow them and the Fair Folk wish no unwelcome visitors.

When they reached the edge of the tree line they hunkered down in a dry ditch and surveyed the village and the farmland down below. Farmer Campbell was working in his hen house, obviously fixing the damage of the previous night. His wife was coming out of the barn with a bucket in her hand. You could just see splashes of milk spilling out every now and then as she walked. The collie dog was chained outside waiting to be called to work the farm beasts. The village looked very peaceful. A horse and cart stood outside the church and a human was wandering about in the graveyard. It was too early for most humans to be out and about. Humans are lazy creatures in comparison to Fair Folk.

"There's no fox's tail," Hamish said.

"What?" asked Misty.

"There's no fox's tail hanging up. When a fox is caught the farmer kills him and hangs his tail up on the fence to deter other foxes from coming to the hen house. There is none, therefore the farmer hasn't caught the fox. Why not?" asked Hamish.

"Lots of reasons I expect. The fox just got away, probably." Misty answered.

"That doesn't happen very often. I think there is something funny going on there."

"Just because a fox got away!" replied Misty.

"If the fox got away, where are the night shift? They would have escaped too, wouldn't they? It's not usual for a fox to attack us is it?

No, there's something funny going on down there." finished Hamish.

They fell into silence, each considering Hamish's point of view at the same time scanning the countryside for any sign of the night shift. Fair Folk are very difficult to see due to their size and the green clothes they wear. Their camouflage is perfect and it usually takes the excellent eyesight of their own folk to spot them.

"Excuse me," a high pitched voice came from behind them almost making them jump out of their skins. "Excuse me, I need your help."

The voice belonged to a robin. It was a robin they both recognised as they had helped her last Spring when humans had thrown stones at her nest. She had tried to defend her newborn chicks from the attack and had her wing broken by one of the stones. Hamish and Misty had made a splint, bandaged her wing and looked after her until it became strong again.

"Hello there," said Hamish. "I can see blood on your feathers. Are you in trouble again? "

"Oh no! It's not my blood," answered the robin. "I rescued one of your folk at dawn. He's in a bad way. I think he has broken his leg and it is bleeding badly. I've been huddled up beside him, trying to keep him warm. I've been waiting for you to come along and help me. He is too big for me to carry, you see. "

"Where is he? He could be my brother!" yelled Hamish.

"Follow me, please," replied the robin as she turned and hopped back into the undergrowth.

Hamish and Misty immediately began to crawl after her, under bushes and through the new shoots of bracken sprouting out of the ground. It was not really that far but it seemed to take hours not minutes to Hamish who was desperate to find Calum. Eventually the robin stopped hopping and scurried under a bramble bush.

"He's in here!" she chirruped.

The duo followed, unheeded by scraped faces and arms as the bramble protected itself against intruders. The deeper into the bush, the darker it became. Lying right at the root of the bush they could see a figure outlined against the first grown branches. Hamish scrambled nearer until he looked down into the dirty, scraped face of his brother.

8

"Calum!   Can you hear me Calum?" he whispered.

An agonised smile appeared on the face. "You took your time getting here didn't you? Now take me home. I need to be mended and talk to Chief Fernlea. Things are not as they should be on Campbell's farm," said Calum.

Chapter 3

Hamish looked down into the depths of his barley broth occasionally stirring it round with his horn spoon. For the first time in many a long year he just could not eat! Worry and confusion dominated his thoughts. The last time he felt like this was when his parents were killed by the old barn owl that used to live in Campbell's barn. It too, now departed into the next world.

"Campbell's Farm, Campbell's Farm," he thought, "that's the place to start to untangle the mystery of Calum's attack."

Calum was in bed, in the sleeping chamber. He had muddled thoughts too. Heather the healer had been waiting for him when Hamish and three others carried him home on a stretcher. He couldn't remember who else had actually carried the stretcher. Misty had run to fetch them, brought them back to the bramble bush and then issued orders all the way home. Heather had cleaned his wounds and straightened his leg. It had indeed been broken just as the robin had said to Hamish. It was now incased in two wooden splints tied round with bandages to keep the bones in place. It didn't hurt quite so much now. Heather had rubbed a soothing salve over all his cuts and scratches. She had given him a warm drink to help him to sleep.

He felt ever so sleepy, but Chief Fernlea would be here soon to listen to his story of what had happened – he should stay awake! Several minutes later Calum was sound asleep. The hot drink had achieved its aim. All was quiet in the sleeping chamber. Calum did not even snore.

In the cooking chamber Hamish was continually stirring his broth but the horn spoon never reached his mouth. It just continued going round and round, almost making the barley dizzy! The thoughts in Hamish's head were also going round and round but far from making him dizzy, events were getting clearer. He tried to list them in order.

"Campbell's Farm this morning, Farmer Campbell in the hen house, Mistress Campbell milking the cows, dog chained up in the yard, no fox's tail hanging up. The clue was there, he just couldn't see it.   There was something odd there; he could feel it in his bones."

Suddenly he jumped up, the stool he had been sitting on overturned and landed with a crash behind him. He banged down his fist, spilling barley broth over the scrubbed white surface of the table.   Hamish did not even notice.

"I've got it, Misty. I've got it! I know what was so odd this morning!" he shouted.
"If you've got it, would you like to share it?" asked a deep voice from the doorway.

Hamish looked up and saw Chief Fernlea coming towards him. Hamish had been so deep in concentration he had not been aware of the Chief being in his home. He stared, and slowly began to sit down. Luckily Misty had picked up his stool and replaced it behind Hamish or he would have fallen onto the floor. Chief Fernlea sat down at the table opposite Hamish and Misty.

"What do you have to tell me?" asked Chief Fernlea quietly.
"I think, I think, I think I know the reason our kin was attacked at Campbell's farm," stuttered Hamish.
"Just tell me what your thoughts are. It may help us to understand why this attack took place."
"Well," said Hamish, "I was confused by there being no fox's tail hung up to show that the farmer had killed the fox which had raided the hen house. He surely would have caught him, wouldn't he? If a fox was near the hen house, the dog would have barked to warn the farmer. If the dog had barked, Calum and the others would have been alerted too, and left. They wouldn't have been there when the fox got in.

How did the fox get in anyway? Foxes don't usually attack us. Why did this fox attack us? Maybe it wasn't a fox at all but the farmer's collie dog. That's why it didn't bark, it was the attacker! If it was the dog, why did the patrol report a fox? That part is still a mystery to me."

"What you are saying does make sense, Hamish," answered Chief Fernlea. "While you were eating and thinking about this puzzle, I was in the sleeping chamber talking to Calum. He told me he saw black and white fur on the belly of the fox. The patrol from the farm saw a fox enter the hen house through the door. They also saw Farmer Campbell *with* the fox. I think the farmer dressed his dog in the fox's skin and led him in to attack us. The mystery is why? It is our right to forage from the humans. We have been doing this for hundreds of years. It is our payment in return for healing their sick animals, even if they don't always know we do this, as we go to the farms at night while the farmers are asleep.

I am going now to discuss this with the members of the Council. Calum is sleeping now; you should eat your broth Hamish. Leave this business to the Council. We will decide what happens next."

Chief Fernlea rose from the table and crossed the room to talk to Granny who was making pancakes on the girdle at the fireside.

"When Calum is awake you will have to tell him that his friends from the patrol have not yet returned. Hopefully, we will find them as we did Calum himself," he said.

He was just about to leave the cooking chamber when he was startled by a metallic ringing in the room. Above his head he could see the nails of the chimes rattling together. The chimes were not ringing for pleasure; someone at Headquarters had pulled the strings that were attached to chimes in every home on the hill.

"Intruder alarm!" shouted Hamish.

Chief Fernlea ran from the chamber to get back to Headquarters. Hamish and Misty too, jumped up and ran. They were making for their lookout post. Each thinking the same thought. "Who was the human intruder?"

Chapter 4

Hamish scrambled up the tree root staircase and cautiously looked out over ground level. Seconds later, Misty appeared beside him. Both looked around and upwards towards the sky before venturing out. Chief Fernlea was nowhere to be seen. He must already be at Headquarters receiving information on the intruder.

Hamish's home was about six trees down from Headquarters and Misty was his neighbour as well as his work partner. Several years ago a branch had been ripped from Hamish's tree during a severe storm and landed between the two homes. Autumn leaves had gathered behind it, blown there by the wind. Into this natural location, Hamish and Misty's lookout post had been built. Misty's mother had sewn some fallen Autumn leaves onto an old woollen blanket which provided a canvas or tent like structure, when secured behind the branch. Numerous more leaves had gathered over and around it providing perfect camouflage. Peering out of a crack between the canvas and the branch they had an ideal view of anyone who may come up the hill, on their side. They waited. . . . .

Chief Fernlea was met with a hive of

activity as he entered Headquarters. Lookouts were all around the outside perimeter of this tree. He did not see them, he felt their presence and knew they were ready to defend. .... if necessary! Making his way to the Council chamber, he was passed by many messengers scampering around, collecting and delivering information. Inside the Council chamber, five gnomes were standing around a large table in the centre of the room. Fergus, Donald, Torquil, David and McBeth had arrived already. They were unfolding a map and laying it out. It could have been a table cloth as it almost covered the entire surface of the table. Fergus was opening a wooden box from which he took out an acorn cup.

"Bring me up to speed on the intruder!" demanded Chief Fernlea, his face as red as his hair.
"We have had several reports from the north-west side of the hill," answered Fergus. "It appears an adult male is making his way up towards us. We are preparing to plot his route from the village to wherever he intends to go."
"Good," replied Chief Fernlea, "let's get started."

The map was now ready and Fergus laid his acorn cup down.
"He was first spotted here, not far from the Manse House. At this point it was not

determined where he was going. It has since been reported that he has passed patrols, here, here, and here."

Each time Fergus said, "here", he took another acorn cup from his box and placed it upon the map.

"He is definitely heading towards us," said Donald.

At that moment a small gnome rushed in and spoke to the gnome at the far end of the table, then rushed out again.

"He's here now," said Torquil, placing his finger on the edge of the tree line. "No doubt about it, he's coming here!"

Down in the lookout post, Hamish and Misty sat, without speaking, all focus directed on the outside world beyond the crack in the canvas. Suddenly there appeared a moving black object on the horizon. Hamish felt Misty's elbow dig into his ribs. When he turned to look at her he saw her eyes were as big and round as the harvest moon and her finger was shakily pointing towards the crack in the canvas. He nodded. They both watched as the shape became larger and more elongated taking up the outline of a man! It was coming closer; in fact it was coming straight towards them! He was completely dressed in black. He carried a stick which he lent on occasionally to catch his breath. It was not Farmer Campbell as Hamish had first thought. This man was not dressed in farm work clothes. He wore a black coat, breeches and walking shoes and had a black hat perched on his head. The only other colour this man wore was a white circle around his neck.

He was really close now. Hamish felt sure that the man would be able to hear his heart beating so loudly in his chest. The man stopped right beside their lookout post. Misty reached out and clung to Hamish's hand. Hamish held his breath. They could hear the man panting. All they could see were his feet. A tiny spider crawled out of the leaf litter, over his shoe and began its journey up the man's leg. Hamish and Misty sat transfixed, clinging onto each other and barely breathing. The man, with spider in tow, moved on.

It was several minutes before either Hamish or Misty moved. They then turned and looked out of the other side of the canvas. The man was making directly for Headquarters. They couldn't warn Chief Fernlea but he would already know as one of the lookouts nearer the tree would have scurried inside to inform the Council. Still holding onto their breath, Hamish and Misty watched as the man circled Headquarters several times before sitting down, leaning against the trunk of the tree. He was staring right at their branch. They watched as the man reached inside his coat and pulled out a silver flask from which he began to drink. Having quenched his thirst he replaced it inside his coat again. He fumbled inside the other side of his coat. This time he produced a pair of spectacles which he opened out and perched on the bridge of his nose. He felt around inside his coat for a third time before producing a black book. He settled himself comfortably and began to read.

As the sun moved round in the sky, a sunbeam suddenly illuminated the man with the book. Hamish could see something gold glinting on the cover of the book. It was golden. As the sun moved on a little and as Hamish concentrated on the golden shape he could see it was the shape of a cross.

As the sun began to sink behind Ben Lomond the man closed his book, replaced it inside his coat, lifted his stick, stood up and began to walk towards their lookout post again. This time he did not stop but continued walking until they lost sight of him.

"Well what do you make of that?" asked Misty. "I really don't know," replied Hamish, "but one thing is for sure, Chief Fernlea and the Council will have plenty to impart to us soon!"

Chapter 5

Hamish stumbled and almost lost his footing on the root staircase of his home. He was exhausted! It *had* been a long day. His stomach rumbled reminding him it needed to be filled. He pushed his tired feet forward until they reached the cooking chamber. There, he gratefully sank onto a stool at the table. He looked across the room and saw Granny sitting in her favourite chair at the fireside. She unhooked a ladle from the wall beside her and began stirring a large black pot which was suspended over the fire.

"You're fair done in, so you are," said Granny, "and starving too, for you've had nout to eat since this morning. A bowl of barley broth, some oatcakes and a good long sleep in your cosy bed, that's what you need. Then you can tell me all that's been happening and what the Chief said at the meeting."
"You're right as always," replied Hamish, "but tell me first, how is Calum?"
"Calum has been sleeping like a hedgehog in hibernation since you left. He'll be furious to know he's missed all the excitement."
"That he will," answered a sleepy Hamish.

At Headquarters, the five members of

the Council stood around the table. Torquil gathered up the acorn cups while David marked their vacant spot with a piece of charcoal. Chief Fernlea entered as Donald hung the map onto the wall behind him. Behind the Chief came a messenger gnome. He carried a tray on which had been placed a bowl of shortbread, six horn tumblers and a metal jug containing elderberry wine.

"It's going to be a long night. We have much to discuss. This will fortify us through till dawn," declared Chief Fernlea.

The messenger laid the tray down on to the table and began to pour the wine into the six tumblers. Chief Fernlea indicated with his hand that they should all sit down.

"Do you think we managed to dispel any fears the clan may have?" asked Donald.
"I think the meeting went well. It was important to gather the clan together after the intruder today. He did us no harm. He appeared to just read his book," replied The Chief.
"I feel he invaded our privacy which is really not on!" declared Fergus.
"I fear if the villagers see him coming here, they may follow," said McBeth.
"During the day we have chores to do. The messengers have to deliver food from the night foraging to all the households. They cannot get

on with their work if humans are here," said the ever practical David.

"He's quite right! We don't want humans here stopping us from going about our business!" shouted Fergus.

"I think we should calm down," replied Chief Fernlea. "After all it was one human on one day. He may never come here again. He hadn't come before had he? You know as well as I do that humans don't often follow routine. They appear to have sudden impulses to do things they never repeat."

"How do you know he hasn't been here before? There was something familiar about him," said Torquil, thoughtfully.

"We haven't had any humans poking their noses in up here for decades!" shouted Fergus.

"I know that," replied Torquil. "I just feel there is something familiar about him. I'm going to think about it and maybe it'll come to me."

"As I stated at the meeting, we will continue our routines as before," said Chief Fernlea. "The night patrols are out on duty now. They will not be foraging at Campbell's farm tonight though. It may be too dangerous after last night. Tomorrow the day patrols will circulate as usual. All patrols will have to be vigilant both for intruders and for Rusty and Dusty who have still not returned."

"That's another thing!" yelled Fergus. "What are we going to do about Campbell's farm? We need food! We need to forage! Food stocks are at their lowest in Spring before things start to grow again. We need food to survive!"

"May I suggest," began Torquil, "that we have a patrol on special watch as near as we can to Campbell's farm? It may help us to understand why this farmer has set his dog upon us. Is it agreed that it was his dog not a fox as we first thought?"

"From the evidence Calum gave us, together with Hamish's theory, I think we can be justified in saying that it was his farm dog dressed in a fox's skin," replied Chief Fernlea.

"I want to know why!" demanded Fergus.

"I think that by having a special watch patrol, day and night, we may be able to answer your question then," answered David.

"Good," said Fergus. "I'm not happy at all these disruptions to our daily life."

"I agree. They make me feel very nervous," said McBeth.

"We shall just have to be patient," said Chief Fernlea. "In the meantime let's finish this jug of wine and get to bed. Dawn cannot be far away."

"I think two members of the Council should be here at all times. We should not all go to sleep at the same time." voiced a worried McBeth.

"Good point. We shall begin straight away," concluded Chief Fernlea.

The words had no sooner left the Chief's lips when a messenger burst into the chamber.

In his haste, he tripped himself up, fell down and rolled across the floor, only stopping when he bumped into the Chief's chair. The six faces of the Council stared at him.

"Why have you burst into this meeting in such a way?" demanded Chief Fernlea.
"I beg your pardon," apologised the messenger. "It's Rusty and Dusty! They're here! They are not hurt, but they stink!"

Chief Fernlea and the other members of the Council rose as one being and ignoring the messenger who was rubbing his sore leg, walked out of the Council chamber and into the entrance foyer. They could smell them long before they could see them! Rusty and Dusty, Calum's companions from the night before were trying to stand to attention in front of the Chief. It was a difficult task as they appeared to be covered from head to foot in what can only be described as a cow's pancake!

"We are very pleased to see you," began Chief Fernlea, "but what on earth has happened to you?"
"Well," said Rusty. "A fox came into the hen house while we were collecting eggs and attacked us. It sprang at Calum and we could not help him. Funny, the door was open and we made a bolt for it. We have been hiding out in a ditch waiting for nightfall to go and rescue Calum."

"A big cow came and relieved itself on us. We were so well hidden it didn't see us," moaned Dusty.

"Never mind that," said Rusty. "We haven't been able to get near the hen house as Farmer Campbell is still working around his farm. He's an odd human so he is. Do you know what he's doing? He's digging big holes! All the way round his farm. Big holes! He's been at it all day!"

"How peculiar!" said Fergus. "I want to know why he is doing that!"

Chapter 6

As dawn broke over the village and a new day began, Mistress MacLeod was awake. The pain in her joints woke her early every morning. Her arthritis made getting up, washed and dressed a difficult and painful process. It was a good twenty minutes later before she hobbled into her kitchen to face the day. She had soaked her oatmeal for her porridge the previous night but she felt she'd rather have a boiled egg this morning. She opened the press and took out the dish she usually kept her eggs in. Empty! She'd forgotten she used the last one yesterday. Porridge it would have to be!

As she stirred the oatmeal round the pot with her spirtle, she thought how things had changed in her life recently. Her husband had died last year and long ago her children had departed the village to find work in the towns. She lived alone in her wee croft now.

She thought again about the lack of a boiled egg. She had had no problems with running out of eggs before. She had always kept about six hens, but over the past two months a fox had taken them one by one. Farmer Campbell had come and shot the fox and taken him away. She had been left with only one hen – Old Chookie.

The fox wasn't daft, he had taken the younger, more tender hens first. Four weeks ago Old Chookie had died too. She had gone out one evening to shut up the hen house for the night and found the old hen lying in its doorway. She had picked her up and laid her in the dairy, the coolest place in the house. Her hands were very painful after doing the day's chores so she decided she would pluck her the next day.

The next morning when she entered the dairy, her mind set on the job to be done, she found that Old Chookie had already been cleaned and plucked ready for her to cook. The Fair Folk! They were so kind. It was not the first time she had woken to find some chore had been completed during the night. It was as if they knew when her arthritis was at its worst. She had never seen them though. She would have liked to thank them for their kindness but they were obviously too shy to be seen in the daytime by people. She imagined Old Chookie's feathers stuffed into a quilt to keep them warm. That was all the payment they would take in receipt of their hard work. As she poured her porridge into a bowl and sat down to eat, she decided she would go along and see if Farmer Campbell could get her a couple of hens. It would be nice to have a freshly laid egg for breakfast again.

Later that morning Mistress MacLeod

found herself at the road end leading into Farmer Campbell's farmhouse. Although not far from her croft, it had taken her almost half an hour to walk there, taking several rests on the way. She was surprised to find Farmer Campbell stamping back and forth looking very agitated.

"Good morning," she said, "a fine Spring day is it not? I'm surprised you're not out in your fields sowing barley."
"I have other things to deal with first," he snapped.
"Why have you dug all these big holes?" she asked, noticing them for the first time.
"To plant trees!"
"Trees? Fruit trees, do you mean?"
"Aye, sort of. They fruit in the Autumn."
"What kind of fruit?" she enquired.
"Rowans!"
"Rowans! You can't plant rowans! You know what powers they have!"
"That's why I'm planting them!" he retorted. "All the way round my farm they will be!"

At that moment , Reverend Kirk came along. He halted his cart beside Mistress MacLeod and Farmer Campbell.

"Good morning," he called down to them. "How are you both today?"
An indignant Mistress MacLeod stabbing her

fore finger in the direction of the farmer almost shouted at the Minister "He's planting rowan trees!"

"It's my farm. I'll do what I like!" yelled Farmer Campbell.

"You can't! It's not fair to them and you know it," Mistress MacLeod shouted back at him.

"It's not fair *to them*. You mean it's not fair to *me*!"

By this point Reverend Kirk had jumped down from his cart and allowed his horse to graze on the grass verge. "Now, now, now," he began. "Let's just take a deep breath and calm down. I'm sure we can sort this out."

"We can," answered Mistress MacLeod. "It's easy! He fills in these holes and doesn't plant the trees."

"I'm planting them!" argued Farmer Campbell.

"Why are you planting rowan trees around your farm, Farmer Campbell, and why are you not pleased about this Mistress MacLeod?" asked Reverend Kirk.

"I'm sick to death of working my fingers to the bone to feed those lazy, thieving wee faery folk up on the hill," answered the farmer.

Mistress MacLeod gave a loud gasp. Without thinking she punched Farmer Campbell on the nose and yelled, "Don't ever call them that word. It's disrespectful. They are neither lazy nor thieves. They work hard to help us and only take a little payment in return for their labours. If you plant rowan trees round your farm, I'll….

I'll….. I'll never talk to you again!" she finished and turned on her heel and marched off as best as her arthritis would allow.

"Well, too bad. I'm doing it!" Farmer Campbell shouted after her.

"Maybe we could talk about this," said Reverend Kirk. "I'm sure we could come to some arrangement. The Fair Folk wont be able to come onto your farm with rowan trees all the way round. You know they cannot do that. They do us no harm after all. As Mistress MacLeod says they actually help us."

"Well, well, well," began Farmer Campbell. "You, Reverend Kirk, a good Christian Minister, telling me it is fine for folk to steal when the commandments say we must not! What a turn up for the books that is. Now if you will allow me to say good morning to you, as I see the cart coming over the bridge with my trees. I need to plant as many as possible before the day is out."

Reverend Kirk returned to his horse, picked up the reins and climbed back onto his cart. What had begun as a beautiful morning had turned out to be gloomy. It was not the weather though but his thoughts that made this change. He felt quite puzzled. Who was correct here, Mistress MacLeod or Farmer Campbell? Perhaps he would take a walk up Doon Hill this afternoon to clear his thoughts and see if God could help him find a solution to this problem and allow two old friends to speak to each other again.

Chapter 7

As the stars closed their eyes to sleep and the sun awoke in the east, Hamish and Misty were crawling into a hole at the bottom of a dry stone dyke opposite Campbell's farm gate. Chief Fernlea had sent them on a special assignment. They must stay there, hidden in the wall, camouflaged by the swaying daffodils until dusk when they would be relieved by Rusty and Dusty. They would then return to Headquarters and report their observations.

The sun had only half appeared from behind the hills when they spotted Farmer Campbell coming out of his farmhouse and start walking down the track to the farm gate. When he arrived there he opened it, closed it behind him and walked out onto the main road, only steps away from Hamish and Misty's hiding place. He looked down the road towards the bridge, and then retraced his steps to the farm gate. He leant against it, taking a pipe from his pocket and lighting it before walking out and looking down the road again. He stamped back to the gate and looked around.

"What do you think he is up to?" asked Misty. "He must be waiting for someone from the hamlet, over the bridge," replied Hamish.

"There's someone coming this way," said Misty, pointing in the other direction.
"I think that is Mistress MacLeod. I wonder why she is up and about so early this morning."

They observed the two humans meet and strike up a conversation. They listened carefully.

"Horse and cart coming over the bridge now. What a busy place today," stated Hamish.

They watched the cart come closer and as the human jumped from it to join Farmer Campbell and Mistress MacLeod, Misty recognised him.

"That's the intruder!" she whispered.
"Ssh!" said Hamish," listen to what they are saying."

They witnessed the whole episode between the three humans.

"Did you see that?" exclaimed Hamish. "Mistress MacLeod can surely pack a punch, can't she?"
"I know, but keep paying attention," replied Misty. "Look a second cart is coming over the bridge and it is loaded with young trees!"

They watched as Farmer Campbell greeted this new human by smiling and shaking

his hand. They watched as both humans unloaded the cart. They watched as Farmer Campbell dug deep in his pocket and gave something to the other human. They watched that human jump onto his cart and drive away back over the bridge. They watched all afternoon as Farmer Campbell planted one tree into each of the big holes. They watched as he laughed while he dug and shouted to the winds,
"NO MORE FAERIES ON MY LAND NOW!"

Mistress MacLeod was angry, very angry! What was Farmer Campbell doing? He knew the Fair Folk could not go onto land where rowan trees grew. Some people believe that rowans take away their magical powers. If the Fair Folk do have magical powers they must use them for healing. She had never heard of the Doon Hill Fair Folk doing anything nasty. Maybe Fair Folk in other places did, but not here. They had helped her by plucking Old Chookie, didn't they?

It suddenly struck her why she had gone to see Farmer Campbell in the first place. She could not ask him to get her some hens now – she'd said she would not talk to him anymore! Her thoughts became centred on that problem. Where could she get eggs from now? Where could she get some hens from? Oh, why did Farmer Campbell have to stir things up? Why could he not leave well alone?

Reverend Kirk was perplexed. What was he going to do about this situation? He'd driven home, stabled his horse, brought supplies from the cart into the Manse without even realising he was doing so. He now paced up and down, up and down from one side of his study to the other. The noise of his boots on the oak floor echoing through the house, disturbing the bats from their slumbers. His thoughts were all over the place. He had heard of people in the Highlands planting rowan trees around their home to protect themselves against the evil of the Fair Folk or Sidhe (shee) as they called them up there. The Wee Folk up on Doon Hill weren't evil, were they? Mistress MacLeod said they helped her, didn't she? Farmer Campbell said they stole from him! Were they really thieves or just taking payment for some work they had done?

He had been intrigued by stories of the Fair Folk since he was a boy, yet he actually knew no more about them now than he had done then. When his father had been the Minister here all these years ago, he would take himself off up the hill to spy on them. He never actually saw any of them but he always felt they were watching him. Now he had returned to Aberfoyle, himself the new Minister, his interest had surfaced again. Had he not walked up there only yesterday? He had wanted to read his Bible in the peace and quiet. Hadn't he?

Had his childhood memories carried him there to seek for them once more? He really was not sure. He would have to walk up there again, today! He was not certain what he would find, but supposing, just supposing he saw one of the Fair Folk for the first time……………………………

Chapter 8

Hamish and Misty were on their way back to Headquarters. The sun was sinking fast, creating an orange-red fire in the sky. Soon the murky gloom of dusk would descend. This was the time when owls awoke from their daily slumbers. This was the time they were at their hungriest. This was the time when Hamish and Misty's assignment was most dangerous.

They kept to the shelter of the dry stane dyke until it reached the Pow Burn. It was then necessary to go up onto the road to be able to cross the bridge. Running water and wet feet hold no attraction for Fair Folk. Hamish poked his head through a hole at the bottom of the dyke.

"Anyone around?" inquired Misty.
"Not a living soul," whispered Hamish in response.

Misty stifled a giggle. That was the same reply Hamish had given when they crossed through the graveyard.

They scrambled across the bridge and dropped down once again into a field. Humans might see them if they remained on the road.

Crossing over the fields provided both the shorter and quicker route to home. The sun had gone down and twilight was upon them. They had to be extra vigilant now. They skirted the bottom of the Manse garden taking advantage of the bushes and shrubs which grew there to camouflage them. They were fast approaching the last leg of their journey to Doon Hill. A quick scarper up the slope from their refuge, across the track and into the protection of the first oak trees. Hamish was becoming aware of his empty stomach. Several hours had passed since he had last eaten. He licked his lips in anticipation of Granny's broth. He could almost taste it.

"Down!" Misty's voice cut through his day dreaming and he felt himself being pulled down into a nearby bramble bush.
"What the............," he began.

Misty clamped one hand quickly over his mouth and with the other pointed over the track to the branches of the closest oak tree. Hamish's eyes followed her pointing finger and located a fully grown tawny owl sitting there waiting for her first meal of the evening to scurry past. He nodded and Misty lifted her hand from his mouth.

"That was a near thing," whispered Hamish.
"She's found an excellent place to spot prey, hasn't she?" returned Misty.

"She certainly has," agreed Hamish, "and we could have been her first dish of the day."

"You may have been, but not me," replied Misty.

"Why me?"

"You're fatter than me. She could not take us both at once so she would have chosen the one with the most meat," grinned Misty.

"Cheeky!" answered Hamish. He knew she was right though - almost. He wasn't really fatter but he had been the one day dreaming about filling his stomach. He kept these thoughts to himself and instead replied, "We will have to stay here and wait until she moves off to another perch. It could be a long wait!"

Misty nodded in agreement.

At Headquarters Chief Fernlea and his council members were around the table once more. The observation map hung on the wall behind them and many more charcoal circles had been added.

"I want to know why this intruder has come again today," demanded Fergus.

"We don't really know why he comes," said Chief Fernlea.

"He's messing up the duties. We cannot get on with normal tasks because we have to sit in look out posts and watch him," shouted Fergus.

"It's what we have to do when intruders come, that has always been the rule," said David.

"I know it's the rule but how are we to distribute food around our homes with him sitting there reading his blooming book," bellowed Fergus.

"With Farmer Campbell playing funny games down there we don't actually have much food to distribute," said Donald.

"That's another thing, where are we going to go foraging now. We need to eat. It's Spring, the land gives us nothing at this time of year. Things are just beginning to grow. We have enough to do without sitting about watching a human reading a book!" insisted Fergus.

"It would help us to know why, wouldn't it?" asked Donald.

"Why! Why! WHY!" shouted Fergus, "we need answers, not more questions!"

"Please calm down Fergus. If we discuss this quietly we may find these answers," pleaded Torquil.

"I think," began McBeth, speaking for the first time, "I think it would help if we knew who this intruder was then we might know why he comes here."

"That's a good point," said Chief Fernlea. "We may also be able to work out if Farmer Campbell's activities are linked to the intruder."

"Do you think the two may be connected?" asked Fergus.

"It is always possible," replied the Chief.

"Maybe these two humans are a team. They want to starve us out of our home," said McBeth anxiously.

"I think we will have to wait and hear Hamish and Misty's report first. What they have seen today may help us piece together a picture of what we have to face," said Donald.

"That's a good idea," replied Chief Fernlea. "They should be back any moment."

"Actually it's dark now. They should have already returned," said Torquil.

"They are never late back from patrol. Hamish's stomach wouldn't allow it. I will go and check with the other patrols, perhaps they have seen them," replied Donald.

"Something awful has happened to them. They're doomed! I just know it!" declared a worried McBeth.

Chapter 9

Hamish awoke to a sharp jabbing pain in his cheek. He nervously opened one eye. What he saw was not his Granny as he had expected but a red face containing two black beady eyes and a sharp, narrow beak. Instantly he remembered he was not at home in his cosy bed as he should be but out on patrol, unable to return home because of the tawny owl.

"I hope you two are not on look out duty, curled up sleeping there under my breakfast bush like two hedgehogs in hibernation. Have you got no work to do? I have to get back to my eggs. Get off my worm patch!"

The red face, two beady eyes, sharp narrow beak and cheeky voice belonged to the robin that had taken care of Calum. Hamish scrambled up and kicked Misty gently with his foot to wake her up.

"Time to get up Misty!" he said.
A groan came back in reply. He tried again.
"Misty, get up! We've been here all night and we need to report back to Headquarters."
"Has the owl gone now?" she asked groggily.
"That old tawny owl has been gone for hours. She is stuffed full of mice and voles. She's a

good hunter, you know. Lucky for you pair you got into this bush or she would have had you for supper too," declared the robin.

"I'll just give myself a wee shake and I'll be ready to go," answered Misty.

"We're sorry to have disturbed your breakfast Robin," Hamish apologised. "We'll get off now and thanks for waking us up or the night patrol would have been home before us. Cheerie Bye."

Hamish grabbed Misty by the hand and dragged her out from under the bush and up the slope to the track. He looked up to the tree where the tawny owl had been. Nothing, absolutely nothing! It appeared only the robin was up and about at this time of the morning. Chief Fernlea would be worried. They needed to get back and report their findings of the previous day. Haste was now the word of the moment and Hamish ran all the way back dragging a very sleepy eyed Misty behind him.

Hamish and Misty were not the only ones who had not slept in their own beds. At Headquarters Chief Fernlea and all the members of the Council had stayed awake anxiously waiting for Hamish and Misty's return.

Chief Fernlea was deep in thought. It would soon be sunrise and Rusty and Dusty would be back. Had they relieved the day patrol as instructed? Had they seen or spoken to Hamish and Misty? Were they at the look out post when Rusty and Dusty got there? Had something befallen Hamish and Misty which had prevented their return?

Suddenly a messenger burst into the chamber. He tripped and fell, rolling along the floor and only halting when he bumped into Chief Fernlea's chair.

"You again! That is the second time you have burst into this room and rolled along the floor. Can you not knock and walk in like normal folk?" asked Fergus.

"Begging your pardon, Sir," answered the messenger, looking round at all the faces of the Council before addressing the Chief. "Hamish and Misty have just returned. Looks like they've been dragged through a hedge backwards, if you ask me."

"Show them in at once! Stop dawdling! Do you think we have stayed here all night for nothing! Get on with it!" shouted Chief Fernlea.

"Very sorry Sir, very sorry," answered the messenger at the same time backing off towards the door. It was not usual for Chief Fernlea to shout and the messenger had no wish to incur the temper of his chief.

A very tired and bedraggled Hamish and Misty entered the Council chamber. Both were dirty and had scratches on their hands and faces. Their eyes were glazed and sunk into their sockets. Hamish's stomach began to rumble and the noise of it seemed to echo around the room. He hoped the Chief and the Council could not hear it.

"Thank goodness you have returned," said Chief Fernlea, "we have been most concerned."
"Where on earth and all that is mystical, have you been?" demanded Fergus.
"Are you hurt?" asked McBeth.
"What is going on down in the village that has caused you to be so late returning?" inquired David.
"Bide your time. Let them sit down first. Get them a hot honey drink and some toast. They looked exhausted. Once they have been suitably fortified they can give us a clear report of what has been happening. Something obviously has or they wouldn't be late and in this state would they?" asked the ever practical Donald.

A messenger was called and dispatched to fetch breakfast. Hamish and Misty gratefully sat down on a wooden bench and began to collect their thoughts. Once fed and watered, they reported the scene at Campbell's farm including the part played by Mistress MacLead. Fergus hooted with laughter and even Chief Fernlea allowed a smile to cross his face. Misty then continued the story revealing the identity of the intruder.

"I knew it, I knew it," exclaimed Torquil.

"Knew what?" asked Fergus.

"I knew I'd seen that face before. I just couldn't place him. The intruder has been here before, many years ago, when he was a young boy. He came almost every day in Summer. He was always poking things with a stick, turning over windfall branches and prying into holes. It was almost as if he was looking for *us*!"

An eerie silence descended around the chamber at Torquil's words. A human coming with the intention of finding them was extremely serious. What would a human do if he saw them? What if he caught one of them?

"Hamish and Misty, you have done well, you may go home to your beds. You are excused patrol duty today. The Council will now have an emergency meeting. Events are more complex and dangerous than we imagined. All Fair Folk will be called to Headquarters when we have reached a decision on what action we should take," said Chief Fernlea.

Hamish and Misty were glad to be going home to bed but whether they would be able to sleep or not was another question. They walked silently home, each deep in their own thoughts. Owls seemed less frightening than what they may have to face in the near future.

"What is Granny going to say to all this," was Hamish's thoughts as he stumbled down the tree root staircase of his home and was welcomed by the smell of newly baked oatcakes.

Chapter 10

"Is that you Hamish? At long last, I've been so worried about you. After what happened to Calum, I've been thinking all sorts," said Granny as she heard movements on the staircase.

"It's me, Granny. Don't fret, I have lots to tell you but I'm starving. Can I have something to eat first?" answered Hamish as he plodded into the cooking chamber.

Granny turned from the girdle where she had been baking oatcakes and stared at Hamish. He was sprawled across the table, arms folded out in front of him and resting his head on the make shift pillow they made.

"Look at you! You're worn out like an old rag fit for the coup. Let's get some porridge into you before anything else," declared Granny.

"Porridge would be great," agreed Hamish. "I've only had a wee bit toast up at Headquarters since yesterday's lunch."

"A wee bit toast! That's not enough to feed a sparrow!" exclaimed Granny putting a steaming bowl of porridge down in front of her grandson.

After eating two bowls of porridge and drinking three cups of apple tea Hamish felt ready to tell Granny of his adventures. She was sitting on a chair close to the fireside and beckoned to him to draw his chair from the table to sit on the opposite side of the fire facing her. He recounted his journey from the very beginning, missing not one detail. At parts Granny nodded, others she twisted her apron on her knee and gasped. She waited until he had completed his story before she looked him straight in the eye and began to speak.

"Your tale makes me very worried. I can see why Chief Fernlea and his Council have to discuss this situation. It's serious. If the wrong decisions are taken it could be the end of us all," she said gravely.

"I appreciate the seriousness of it all but do you not think Mistress MacLeod skelping Farmer Campbell really funny? An old woman like her too," answered Hamish.

"I suppose so. I might have done it myself though. Him, planting rowan trees, there's no way we can go on his land now and he knows it!" replied Granny.

"Do you think humans know the real story of the rowans though or do they just believe it takes away our *magical* powers?" asked Hamish.

"I don't think they have the sense to know the real reasons," answered Granny.

"Tell me the story again, please," begged Hamish who never tired of his Granny's stories from the distant past.

"Well," she began. "One day long, long ago when the humans were still living in caves, hunting for food and wearing animal skins our Princess decided to have a huge birthday party. All the creatures of the land came except the humans, of course. There was much feasting, drinking, singing and dancing, everyone was having a great time. The King had presented his daughter with a beautiful golden goblet. One of the owls was very jealous of this goblet and wanted it for his own. He flew down and snatched the goblet from the Princess's hand and took off into the sky. The Princess screamed and on hearing that scream her father took up his bow and arrows. He shot down the owl and returned the goblet to the Princess. The chief of owls was not pleased to say the least. After all, one of his clan had been killed. He pulled a small oak sapling from the ground and took it over to where his dead comrade lay. He planted the sapling, mixing its blood with the earth. He stood back and shouted to the King that this tree would grow and become known as a rowan after the name of the dead owl. Its leaves would resemble its feathers and its berries would be as red as the blood spilt that day. He finished by cursing all the Fair Folk. If any of us should cross onto land where this tree grew the owls would take their revenge and massacre us all."

The cooking chamber was silent for a time after Granny finished her story. It seemed to

Hamish that between the owls and the intruder their fate was sealed. It looked like this was the beginning of the end of the Fair Folk of Doon Hill.

"Well sitting here telling stories wont get the work done," said Granny eventually. "Away to your bed Hamish. It will probably be some time before the Chief calls the folks together. You need to get some sleep while you can."

Hamish nodded, rose from his chair and made his way to the sleeping chamber. He doubted he could sleep as he had so many things going on in his head. However, only moments after placing his head on the pillow he fell asleep. Granny, too had many thoughts swirling around in her head but sleep was not for her. She sent up a silent prayer to the Forest Gods that this situation could be resolved without bloodshed and all could go on as before.

Chapter 11

The Council too, knew how serious the situation was becoming. Having dispatched Hamish and Misty homewards, they immediately sat down around the table to discuss the details of the report. Rusty and Dusty had reported a quiet night, therefore they must act only on the information Hamish and Misty had provided. Chief Fernlea was well aware this was the most serious situation his clan had faced since he became Chief. He did not want to come to a wrong decision. In fact there were two events to think about, but were they separate or linked in some way. He suddenly became aware that the Council members were all looking at him, obviously waiting on him to speak and begin the discussion. He decided to angle the conversation around to what they had been thinking. In doing so, it may clarify his own thoughts.

"Well," he began. "It appears we have two different sets of circumstances to deal with here. What are your thoughts on the matter?"
"That Farmer Campbell has to take down his trees and that Robert Kirk should stay in his own home and mind his own business!" declared Fergus instantly.

"How can we make them do anything? We have to look at alternatives," replied David.

"I think we should look at each incident separately and try and find a solution," answered Donald.

"I agree," said McBeth quietly. "I feel we need to look into the food matter first as we all need to eat"

"Farmer Campbell has the biggest farm and therefore became the main source of our foraging. We need to obtain milk, eggs, oats and corn. They are all in short supply in the storage chamber," commented Torquil.

"Where else do you suggest we get these items from then?" asked Fergus.

"We will have to search among the crofts over the river," answered Donald.

"There is only the one bridge for us to cross and it is quite far away from here. The further we have to go the more dangerous it becomes," worried McBeth.

"I know that!" retorted Fergus, "but there is nowhere else is there?"

"Not on this side of the river," agreed Donald. "The humans here only grow a few vegetables and some fruit in their back gardens."

"If only Mistress MacLeod hadn't become so frail. She used to have a cow and some hens," said Torquil.

"Well she has!" Fergus almost shouted.

Chief Fernlea could see the discussion

was becoming a little heated. If tempers got frayed no sensible solution would be found. It was understandable, of course. They were very tired and worried.

"I think you are all correct," he interrupted. "There is no other solution but to cross the river. It will have to be controlled of course. We cannot have patrols wandering all over the place hoping to find some food. Donald, bring out the map of the other side of the river. Let's begin by allocating patrols to possible targets."
"We have to give them something in return for the food," reminded McBeth.
"We will, after we have looked at the map," promised Chief Fernlea.

The next hour was passed deciding which patrols should investigate which crofts. The patrols also had to be given instructions for what to look for. It was no good all of them returning with the same produce. They would also be instructed to look out for some way of returning the favour, a sick animal in need of help, a broken fence to be mended or any wee job around that needed attention. The patrols would have to work at night of course, as humans were about during the daytime. That brought forth the added danger of owls and with Hamish and Misty reporting the sight of a new tawny owl so close to Headquarters, they would have to be vigilant.

"Now we have that all sorted out, what are we going to do about Robert Kirk?" asked McBeth.

"We should lock him up in that Manse of his and throw away the key," replied Fergus.

"Not very practical," said Donald

"We should do nothing, at present," answered Chief Fernlea.

"Nothing!" Fergus did shout this time. "What do you mean; nothing!"

"I think we should just observe his movements for a wee while. See where he goes. See what he does. See what brings him up here," said Chief Fernlea.

"Follow him, you mean. See what makes him tick?" asked David.

"Exactly," replied Chief Fernlea.

"Who do you think are the best trackers and could be spared from the foraging?" asked Donald.

"What about giving Hamish and Misty that duty. They are good at blending in with their background and no one ever hears them going about," suggested Torquil.

"They do give very detailed reports," commented Fergus. "We would miss nothing if they were assigned that task."

"Are we all agreed?" asked Chief Fernlea.

All heads nodded in agreement.

"I think we have achieved remarkable progress and we should all get some food and sleep now. Then we will call the whole clan together and explain to them what has been happening and how we are going to deal with the situation," declared the Chief.

They had all just risen from the table and were making their way out of the Council chamber when they were startled by the intruder alarm chimes. Messenger gnomes and lookouts were scurrying all over the place, running in all directions, like bees round a honey pot.

"I bet it's that Robert Kirk again! Can't he leave us in peace for one day!" demanded Fergus.
"You all go and get some sleep. I'll remain here. If it is Robert Kirk, he probably only wants to sit and read his book again. If not and it is something else, I'll send a messenger to fetch you," said a very tired Chief Fernlea.

Chapter 12

The last few days of warm sunshine had encouraged Spring to erupt into all its natural beauty. The heads of the bright yellow daffodils danced to the birdsong that filled the woods and the hamlet. Hamish wished he could dance to the tunes also but right at that moment it was impossible. At present he and Misty were hiding in the branches of a flowering red currant bush which grew at the side of the Manse's doorstep. They were waiting. They had been waiting since daybreak. Soon the sun would reach its highest point in the sky which would indicate to Hamish that it was time for a mid-day meal. They continued to wait…….

"What do you think he is doing in there?" asked Misty.

"Who knows," answered Hamish. "Maybe he ate too much fruit yesterday and has spent all morning sitting on the chanty!"

"I wish he would come out. I'm getting pins and needles in my legs sitting all cramped up in here," complained Misty.

"I ate too many brambles once and I had to sit on the chanty all morning," Hamish continued.

"Will you be quiet about chanties! Can't you think about something more pleasant?" retorted Misty.

Hamish decided it might be better to say nothing at all. When Misty was fed up she always complained. It did not really matter what topic of conversation Hamish pursued she would grump and moan about it. No, much safer to say nothing. He allowed his attention to focus on the Manse garden in front of him. His eyes were drawn to some bubbling in the pond. He leaned closer, almost falling out of the bush to try and see what was causing this movement.

"What are you trying to do now?" asked Misty irritably.
"Look at the pond," he replied, "it's bubbling."
Misty looked, "so it is. Why is it doing that?"
"It's my children," said a voice from behind the stone urn which stood on the doorstep.
"Who are you? Come out and show yourself!" demanded Hamish.
A large, warty bundle suddenly landed right between them.
"You're a toad," exclaimed Hamish.
"Well I was the last time I looked at my reflection in the water," answered the toad.
"What are your children doing to make the pond bubble?" asked Misty.
"They're hatching," replied the toad. "Lots of little tadpoles taking their first swim and investigating their surroundings and looking for food."
"Don't you help them?" inquired Misty.

"Nope! They're on their own now. I do go along now and again though, just to see how many of them are still alive. Lots of beasties like to eat us, you know. We are very tasty," said the toad proudly.

"Are you not sad when your babies are eaten?" Misty asked.

"I have too many of them to get to know them properly. I have hundreds of them in there. I'm not like a bird, you know. I don't just have two or three and molly coddle them. My babies are independent. Anyway if too many of them survived there would be no room in the pond for me now, would there!" explained the toad indignantly.

Hamish and Misty had no answer to that. There was silence for a time.

Suddenly the toad asked, "What are you both sitting in that bush for?"

"We're waiting for Robert Kirk to come out so we can follow him," Hamish informed him, glad the eerie silence had been broken.

"You'll have a long wait then," came the answer.

"Why?" questioned Misty.

"Why? Today is Saturday, of course," replied the toad.

"What difference does that make?"

"Well, tomorrow will be Sunday then, wont it?"

"We know the days of the week!" retorted Hamish.

"Then you should know that the Reverend will

be writing his sermon for Church tomorrow," answered the toad.

"We don't understand the sermon and the church bit," said a puzzled Hamish.

"Gnomes!" said the toad in an exasperated voice. "Don't they teach you anything up on that hill these days? He's the minister, isn't he? He goes into Church tomorrow and tells all the humans stories about this God chap. He tells them how they should live and take care of each other. He'll be writing it all down at this very moment."

"Is he like a kind of a chief then?" asked Hamish.

"I expect he sort of is. You should really follow him into Church and listen to what he tells them, then you'll get a better picture. You might even increase your knowledge of humans. It appears you're both lacking a little in that department."

Having had her say on the matter, the toad swiftly jumped back behind the stone urn before continuing her way down to the pond to check on the survival rate of her children.

"What a strange, opinionated creature," said Misty.

"A bit cheeky too," agreed Hamish. "Still she did know a bit more about Robert Kirk than we did.

"True," admitted Misty, "and we'll learn a bit

more about him and the other humans if we take her advice and go to the Church tomorrow."

"Sure we will," Hamish replied, " but can we at least eat something now and I don't mean one that toad's tadpoles."

"How about a nice jammy piece," replied Misty pulling a wooden box from her pocket.

"Best idea you've had all day," said Hamish grinning.

The toad was quite correct about Robert Kirk. He did not cross his doorstep all day. Hamish and Misty left their position and made their way home to Headquarters to file their report just as the sun slipped down behind Ben Lomond. A very quiet day had been had except for the meeting with the toad!

Chapter 13

Hamish and Misty set off very early next morning to attend church with the humans. Having reported the events of yesterday, including the encounter with the toad, to the Council, they had then been given a lesson on the Christian beliefs of humans from Donald. Hamish had been reminded that if he had listened more carefully when a youngster in Gnome school, he would already have known about churches and sermons. Hamish had to concede that Donald was correct. Some days he had allowed his thoughts to drift away from the lessons into the woodlands beyond. Now he was caught out and paying the price.

As they tramped through the woody undergrowth, their feet became quite damp as it had rained during the night and the ground was still wet. When they reached the tree line, they halted before crossing the track into the fields on the other side. Hamish gazed in wonder at the sight before him. This was one of his favourite mornings. After night-time rain, he always felt that the countryside looked fresh and clean. It was if the Forest Gods had decided it had been too dusty and had washed everything clean again.

"Are you going to stand there all day or attend to the task we have been assigned?" asked Misty.

"I'm just savouring the newly washed land before the sun dries it all up," answered Hamish.

"Huh!" replied an unimpressed Misty. "You'd be better off concentrating on the job in hand."

Hamish nodded in sad agreement. Misty had already crossed the track and entered the field. Hamish scurried after her. It was a fair distance to the church and they really didn't have time to stand and admire nature's beauty this morning.

All was peaceful as they arrived at the wall surrounding the churchyard. Not a human being or other creature seemed to be around. Donald had stated that they enter by the back as some cold mice had chewed away a section at the bottom of the back door last Autumn.

They skirted the grave stones until they arrived at the back door. Sure enough, a hole had been gnawed at the bottom. Hamish pulled at the chewed wood, making the hole a little larger and more Gnome friendly. They crawled through and found themselves in a small room where the Minister put on his Sunday robes. Donald had said this was called the vestry. If they stayed in this room they would be unable to observe the humans or hear the sermon therefore they must find a dark corner in the main body of the church. They tip toed out of the vestry and allowed their eyes to search for a good hiding place.

"What about on that shelf, behind the books?" asked Hamish helpfully.
"No, they are the Psalters. They sing from them," replied Misty.
"What about behind these big cushion things beside the front door?" asked Hamish.
"No, these are kneeling cushions. The rich humans will pick them up as they come in and take them to their pew," answered Misty.
"Are you tired?" enquired Hamish.
"No, what makes you ask that?"
"You said, phew."
"I said, pew actually, as in their benches, where they sit!" retorted Misty.
"Oh," said Hamish, "sorry."

Hamish looked around again. He could tell Misty was feeling annoyed with him. It was obvious his knowledge of churches was still lacking.

"I know," stated Misty. "Over there, in that corner to the side of the pulpit. There are a heap of curtains we could crawl under. They must have taken them down for Spring cleaning."

Hamish thought he'd better follow Misty, mainly because he couldn't remember what a pulpit was. How did she know about Spring cleaning curtains anyway? He was quite certain Donald hadn't said anything about Spring cleaning.

They settled themselves comfortably, peeking out from underneath to see what was going to happen. They didn't have long to wait until the first human appeared. Soon a steady stream of humans followed and all sat down waiting for the arrival of Reverend Kirk.

After the service Reverend Kirk walked up the aisle to the front door. As was customary, he stood waiting to shake hands with all his parishioners as they left. He hoped they would think about what he had said about sharing what they have with others. His mind had been on the Fair Folk. He was unsure if his congregation had understood the full message of his sermon. As he shook hands with Mistress MacLeod, Farmer Campbell pushed his family past, without shaking the Minister's hand. Everyone in close proximity was able to hear *his* message.

"I'll not be shaking hands with anyone who preaches we should share our goods with these lazy, thieving faery folk!"

Back at Headquarters Chief Fernlea and his Council awaited the return of Hamish and Misty. As time went on, McBeth became more and more anxious.

"Something has happened to them," said a worried McBeth. "They should have been back by now."
"Hamish will have stopped off for a jammy piece," answered Torquil.
"He better not have. I want to know what occurred in that church," stated Fergus, loudly.

A knock was heard at the door and a very timid messenger Gnome entered. He was determined not to rush in and fall over ever again!
"Hamish and Misty," he announced showing them in.

"Come forward and tell us all," said Chief Fernlea.
"The humans sit quietly and listen to the Minister. Every now and again they stand up and sing," began Misty.
"Not very happy songs," interrupted Hamish.
Misty glared at him before continuing. "He told them a story about a man called Jesus who is their God's son."
"Jesus has magic powers," butted in Hamish. "I liked him."

"Let me finish," complained Misty.

"Reverend Kirk told a story about Jesus talking to hundreds of people on a mountain. They were there all day and became very hungry. He didn't have any food to feed them but a small boy said he had five loaves and two fish he could share with them. Jesus took the food and was able to share it with everyone and there was still some left over to take to the poor. He said they should do as Jesus did and share their food with folk who didn't have any. I think he meant us!" finished Misty.

Hamish had nodded all the way through Misty's account and when she stopped to draw breath he took up the story as he saw it. "I told you! This Jesus guy can do magic tricks! How else could he have fed so many people with only five loaves and two fish?"

"The message was to share their food with others," Misty interrupted, "Not, look at me, I'm a magician!"

"Thank you for your report. You may go now," said Chief Fernlea, dismissing them before a full blown argument began.

Hamish and Misty left the Council chamber with Misty scolding Hamish for interrupting her account and for trying to make them look silly. Chief Fernlea waited until they had closed the door behind them and looked towards his Council. Each member had a grin on their faces, even Fergus.

"I think it would seem as if this Reverend Kirk is on our side but I'm not sure. Too many mysterious events have taken place recently. I feel it is time to inform the King and Queen of The Sidhe about what has been going on here. Agreed?" asked the Chief.

"Agreed," chorused the Council.

"Then I will go first thing tomorrow morning," stated Chief Fernlea.

Chapter 14

A sheet of rain greeted Chief Fernlea as he left Headquarters. It was a gloomy day. He could feel the damp penetrate through his oak bark overcoat. Not only was the rain heavy but his heart was heavy too. He had only been down to the Knowe to celebrate on festive occasions. This time was different. He had to ask for an audience with the King and Queen on reasons of security. Only a month ago they had all been looking forward to Spring and now gloom, more gloom and even more gloom!

The Knowe was situated not far from Doon Hill, not much more than a tussock compared with the mountains round about. To the human eye it appeared no more than a grassy hillock, south of the woods. Chief Fernlea knew exactly where on the Knowe he needed to go. On the south side, he stopped. He looked around. He felt inside his overcoat. He brought out something which he then kept in his hand. He bent down and peeled back a curtain of grass. He disappeared under it.

Chief Fernlea stood in front of an old wooden door partly covered with moss. He knocked three times. It was opened almost immediately by an elf. He was similar in size to the Chief but thinner. He had a beautiful face with deep green eyes, pink mouth, a slender nose and pointed ears. He wore green leather boots and a green, flimsy looking tunic which gave him an almost invisible appearance. A green, pointed hat completed his ensemble. He carried a lantern in his hand.

"State your name and your business," said the elf in a sharp tone of voice.
"I am Chief Fernlea of Doonhill. I have come to request an audience with the King and Queen," answered Chief Fernlea.
"Why?" inquired the elf.
"It is on a matter of security. I believe my tribe, and indeed perhaps all of us are at risk," replied the Chief.
"Show me proof of your identity," ordered the elf.

The Chief put forward his hand, uncurling his fingers to show a gold circular disc. An amber coloured Cairngorm stone shone from its centre causing it to produce rays of yellow light which danced in the light of the elf's lantern. Smaller Cairngorm stones highlighted the outside edge of the disc. The area between was made of gold, Sidhe gold, brighter and stronger than human gold. It was engraved with a series of oak trees and acorns. The elf examined the brooch in great detail before returning it to Chief Fernlea.

"This is indeed the badge of office of the chief of the tribe who protects our oak woodlands. You may pass down into the Kingdom. You will be met by the reception elf when you arrive," stated the elf.

Chief Fernlea reached under his overcoat and pinned his brooch back onto his tunic. As the elf stood aside, Chief Fernlea could see a tunnel lit by tapers attached to the walls at regular intervals. The pathway was made of white stones which descended gently down into the bowels of the earth. Several minutes later the Chief arrived in a huge, brightly lit cavern. On his last visits here it was packed with all the tribes of the Kingdom, dancing, singing and feasting to celebrate the Winter solstice. Today it was empty. It felt cold. Again Chief Fernlea felt the gloom in his heart.

"You are Chief Fernlea and you are here to request an audience with the King and Queen on a matter of security. Is that correct?"

Chief Fernlea turned to face the voice. He was met by another elf who was dressed exactly the same as the first one. He did not carry a lantern but rested his hand on the hilt of a sword which hung at his side. Chief Fernlea had no idea from where this elf had appeared. It was as if he suddenly sprouted out of one of the stalagmites at the edge of the cavern.

"That is correct," answered Chief Fernlea.
The elf nodded. "Follow me, please."

Chief Fernlea did as instructed and found himself being shown into a smaller cave. Although deep underground, this cave was as lit as if by sunlight. Facing him sat the King and Queen on their golden thrones. They were much taller than the Chief, as tall as grown humans. They were both extremely beautiful and the Queen wore her long fair hair down over her shoulders. Both wore long tunics of emerald green studded with jewels. Both wore gold crowns on their heads. Both were smiling down at him. This made him feel less nervous about the news he was about to impart.

"Chief Fernlea, you may remove your overcoat. It is not raining in here," said the Queen. Her voice sounded like a burn flowing gently over its gravel bed.
"Thank you," answered the Chief. The elf took his overcoat and hung it over one of the stalagmites in the corner.
"Now then, tell us what has been going on at Doon Hill," said the King.

Chief Fernlea told the royal duo the whole story from Farmer Campbell and his rowan trees to Reverend Kirk and his excursions. Both King and Queen listened carefully, nodding occasionally to him and each other.

"You were right to come and tell us of these strange happenings," said the King, when Chief Fernlea had finished his story.

"Elf Rhyland will give you some refreshments while the King and I discuss this situation. We will call you back when we have reached a decision," said the Queen.

Elf Rhyland led Chief Fernlea into another small cave where a table was set with warm bread, cheese, and a jug of elderflower wine. He sat down and at once began to partake of the food. He had felt so gloomy this morning that he had not eaten breakfast. Telling the King and Queen of his troubles had given him an appetite. He then made himself comfortable and waited. He had no idea how long he would have to wait nor did he have any idea what the King and Queen's solution would be.

He would have been very surprised if he could have heard their conversation. Not even Hamish's imagination could have guessed what the King and Queen had in mind.

Chapter 15

Chief Fernlea was deep in thought as he left the Knowe, so deep in thought that he was unaware of his surroundings. He did not notice that the rain had stopped. Nor did he see the mud and puddles he squelched through until he slipped and almost fell into the trunk of a nearby tree. He had no idea what the Council would make of the King and Queen's decision; in fact he was not sure what he made of it himself. Not in his wildest dreams could he have foreseen this as a solution.

Arriving at Headquarters he made his way down the root staircase and into the entrance chamber. Immediately all the messenger gnomes stopped in their tracks and stared at him, mouths open in disbelief.

"Do none of you have any work to do?" he bellowed at them.

Roused back into activity at his words, one gnome came and relieved him of his overcoat, another removed his muddy boots, and then a third slipped his feet into dry footwear. As Chief Fernlea approached the Council chamber, a fourth gnome anxiously opened the door ready to announce him to the Council.

"Chief Fernlea," declared the gnome. "Chief Fernlea and, and, and…….."

"He's an elf!" snapped the Chief, striding into the chamber.

The Council members stood at once at his entrance, all wearing the same vacant look that the gnomes had worn on his arrival. No one spoke. The Chief proceeded towards the table, the elf following in his wake. The gnome began to close the door.

"Bring a chair for our visitor and place it beside mine," demanded the Chief to the gnome who hastily did as he was bid.

"This is Kee," stated Chief Fernlea. "Now, please sit down."

There was silence. Five pairs of eyes goggled at the Chief.

"Kee has been sent by the King and Queen to help us with the problems we face at the moment," said Chief Fernlea, now speaking in his normal tone of voice.

Kee nodded to the Council as way of a greeting.

Still there was silence.

"Kee will stay with us, here at Headquarters, and entertain Robert Kirk when he arrives. This will help us to continue with our normal duties," continued the Chief.

The wall of silence remained intact.

"The King and Queen feel that if Robert Kirk

understands us more, he will be able to portray this to the other humans," Chief Fernlea paused and looked round at his Council. "Kee will therefore escort him away from Doon Hill and take him down into the Knowe."

The dam burst. Silence flew out of the room. It was replaced by a torrent of questions.

"He's to take him down into the Knowe!" exclaimed Fergus.

"Will he meet the King and Queen?" asked Donald.

"Will he see the Brownies making our bread and stews?" asked Torquil.

Will he meet the Sylvan elves tending the gardens?" questioned David.

"Will he meet the Kobbold Smiths and see them making our weapons out of bronze and gold?" worried McBeth,

"What if he tells all the humans and they all come here!" cried Fergus.

Chief Fernlea held his hand up to quieten them all again before answering, "Kee will be his constant guide. Yes, he will see all the tribes and what they do. He will also meet the human prisoners who work in the quarry. He will be told this is where he will go if he tells the villagers of our secrets."

"How is this going to help us?" inquired Torquil.

"By understanding that we are not lazy nor are we thieves as some of the humans believe," answered Chief Fernlea.

"If he cannot tell what he sees, how can he convince the other humans?" asked Donald puzzled.

"Hamish and Misty have already told us about the stories he tells them in the Church. He is a clever human. He will be able to adapt his stories to include us in the teachings of their God," replied Chief Fernlea.

"How do we know we can trust him?" asked McBeth.

"The King and Queen feel that the more he learns about us, the less curious he will be, therefore he will keep our secrets," responded the Chief.

"I don't agree!" declared Fergus. "The risk is too great."

"The King and Queen have said it is to be," replied David.

"We cannot go against the King and Queen," agreed Donald.

"How are we going to know what he says to the villagers?" inquired McBeth.

"I am going to put Hamish and Misty on to the task. They are already familiar with the inside of the Church. They will go there each Sunday and listen to Robert Kirk's sermon. They will then, of course, report back to us and tell us what is said," answered Chief Fernlea.

"A good idea," said Torquil. "Send them before Sunday so as they can find the best possible hiding place."

"At last, some sense," muttered Fergus to himself.

"If I can just ask another question," began Donald. "What did the King and Queen suggest we do about Farmer Campbell and his rowan trees?"

"They suggest we do nothing. They feel the Weather Gods will take care of the trees. He did plant them during the month of May. Everyone should know that if you plant trees when there is no R in the month then only luck will allow them to survive," stated the Chief.

For the first time since he returned from the Knowe, Chief Fernlea was able to see his Council grinning. He dismissed the Council for a meal break, after which they would call a meeting of all the gnomes to inform them of the reason for Kee's presence. As the Council members filed out of the chamber he could hear Fergus muttering to the others.

"That elf never opened his mouth once, did you notice that?"

Chapter 16

Hamish and Misty were huddled under a bramble bush on the edge of the woods. They were both looking up towards an oak tree wherein sat the tawny owl they had seen some time before when returning from the village. As Summer approaches and the daylight hours lengthen, the tawny owl is forced to feed before darkness falls. He hunts, not only for himself but for his family too.

"I wonder just how long we have to sit here before he decides to go and hunt somewhere else," said Misty.

"We haven't been here very long," answered Hamish. "Besides I like this time of year in the woods."

"I just want to get to the Church and find a good hiding place ready for Sunday. I don't like all this hanging around doing nothing," moaned Misty.

"Close your eyes and breathe in the forest smells," said Hamish.

"Close my eyes! Don't be daft. All I'll smell is the stink of owl feathers before I become breakfast for that bird up there!" exclaimed Misty.

"You close your eyes and I'll watch him up there," replied Hamish.

"No, I'm not doing it. He might fly off and you won't notice," Misty answered.

"You make such a fuss about nothing sometimes. Smell the bluebells. What a magnificent blue carpet they make on the woodland floor. Soon they will all die and it will be green again and you'll have missed it," said Hamish.

"So, I'll miss it! When is that bird going to move?" Misty grumbled.

"Maybe it just needs a bit of a push," said Hamish.

"Right you are," agreed Misty. "You just climb up there and give it a shove then."

"Very funny," answered Hamish. "You haven't seen my new secret weapon!"

"What new secret weapon?" asked Misty curiously.

From a pocket inside his jacket Hamish produced a small bow and three long tapering pieces of wood with green feathers on the end.

"Where did you get that?" asked Misty. "What funny looking arrows!"

"Kee gave it to me. He showed me how to use it last night after our meeting with the Council," answered Hamish.

"Why did he give it to *you?*" Misty inquired.

"So I could protect you from hungry owls," replied Hamish grinning.

"I don't need *you* to protect *me!*" sulked Misty.

"I'm only joking," said Hamish. "It's to create diversions. Look I'll show you."

Misty watched while Hamish dug deeper into his pockets and produced a long piece of thread and some sheep's wool. She was not too pleased that Kee had singled out Hamish for individual attention. They were a team! Kee should have given both of them a bow and special arrows. Still, she was intrigued. She watched as Hamish tied the thread to the end of one of the arrows and then attached some of the wool to the other end of the thread. He then lay down on his stomach and aimed into the bluebells and bracken.

"Watch this," Hamish said. "It will soon get the owl's attention."

Hamish fired his arrow which sped through the undergrowth for quite a distance. Immediately the owl turned his head round to look to where the arrow had caused the movement. Hamish fixed another arrow to his bow and fired again. It appeared to go even further. This time the owl turned his whole body round and leant forward a little to see what was causing the movement. Hamish reloaded and fired for a third time. This time the owl flew off towards the movement and perched on another tree away in the distance.

"He's gone! Let's go," said Misty. She was secretly quite impressed by Hamish's new secret weapon and she could see why only one of them really needed it. She wasn't sure she was ready to tell him that just yet though.

They continued on their way uneventfully, towards the Church. They met no more owls or any humans either. Once again they were able to crawl through the hole at the bottom of the back door. Looking around the main part of the Church they noticed some differences from their last visit. The curtains where they had hidden the last time had gone completely. Dead wild flowers stood in the vase beside the pulpit. The floor was dusty and the wooden pews had lost their shine. There was a musty, damp smell everywhere.

"Where can we hide this time?" asked Hamish, looking around.

"It has to be somewhere that won't be moved as we have to come every Sunday now," replied Misty.

"Look at this," said Hamish who was nosing around in the pulpit. "There is a cupboard here just the right size for one of us. It is so stiff and dirty that it obviously doesn't get used. I could hide in there."

"Good idea," replied Misty. "You could take a wedge of wood with you and jam the door from the inside. No one could open it from the outside and you wouldn't be found supposing they suddenly wanted to open it."

"I'll do that," agreed Hamish. "Let's find a

place for you. It would probably be better if we don't hide in the same place anyway. We can see things from different angles that way."

"Don't you think you can have a wee snooze while you're in there though," said Misty. ""Remember the importance of this assignment."

"No fear," replied Hamish. "I liked that Jesus guy. I want to hear more about him."

It took longer to find Misty a good hiding place. Eventually they decided upon a space behind the wooden panelling where one of the planks was loose and she was able to squeeze in behind it.

"Job done!" said Hamish.

"Not before time. Do you hear human voices?" asked Misty.

"You're right, I do," agreed Hamish.

After exiting the back door and running to hide behind the first gravestone they came to, they observed two humans coming up the path to the front door. One of them carried a brush and a feather duster, the other a mop and bucket.

"Told you," said Misty. "Spring cleaning!"

Chapter 17

As he waited for Hamish and Misty to return from the Church, Chief Fernlea was becoming increasingly worried. Every week day for almost a year now Robert Kirk had met with Kee and been taken down into the Knowe. The Reverend had written notes and painted pictures of all he had seen while on these visits. His sermons too, now frequently involved the Fair Folk and the other tribes living underground. The Council too, were showing concern. It did not seem fitting to question the word of the King and Queen but it would appear that Robert Kirk was not abiding by the conditions that had been set in place.

He continued to wait. Hamish and Misty were later coming back than normal; perhaps the tawny owl was out hunting again. His thoughts drifted off to the other problem they had had a year ago – Farmer Campbell and his rowan trees. The King and Queen had said the Weather Gods would take of it and so they had. It had been a particularly long hot Summer last year. The trees planted farthest away from the river had wilted and died through lack of water. Then, when the October rains came the River Forth had burst its banks as was usual in that month, but the rain was fierce and consistent and the floods much worse than normal. Almost all the trees which had survived were washed away downstream towards Stirling, only two remained. The Chief's thoughts were interrupted by the arrival of the Council.

"Have Hamish and Misty returned from the Church?" asked Donald as they all sat down around the table.
"Not yet," replied Chief Fernlea. "I expect that tawny owl has held them up again."
"I worry about them out in the daylight hours with that owl around, not to mention the fact that they are in among all the humans," said McBeth.
"I'm sure they will take care, just as they always do," commented Torquil.

The conversation was halted by a knock on the door which heralded the entrance of a messenger gnome who announced the arrival of Hamish and Misty. They were both red in the face and panting for breath. They looked as if they had run all the way from the Church.

"Have you been chased by that owl?" demanded Fergus.
"Let them catch their breath first," said David.
"We……. we had to…… to run," puffed Misty.
"It's not the owl," gasped Hamish.
"It's………it's what Robert Kirk said today," exclaimed Misty.

"And………and Mistress MacLeod……..she's dead!" whispered Hamish with a sob so obviously stuck in his throat.

"Take your time," said Chief Fernlea kindly. "Just begin at the beginning."

"Well the service started in the usual way and they all sung a hymn and said a prayer," began Hamish. "Then Robert Kirk announced that Mistress MacLeod had died yesterday and there would be a funeral service on Tuesday."

Fergus glowered, "get on with it will you," he said.

Hamish looked vexed.

Misty continued, "He told a story about Jesus healing a sick girl and he said if they had had healers like Heather, Mistress MacLeod might not have died!"

"You mean, our Heather the Healer?" inquired Donald.

"Yes," stuttered Hamish. "He told them we have magical cures which we make ourselves and he had seen Heather making them."

"He's gone too far this time. What are we going to do about it?" shouted an irate Fergus, standing up and banging his fist on the table.

"Sit down Fergus!" commanded Chief Fernlea in a loud voice.

Fergus sat down. "Sorry," he muttered.

"We will tell Kee immediately. He will have to report this to the King and Queen," said Chief Fernlea.

"Where is Kee?" asked Torquil.

Kee had this unnerving way of suddenly appearing out of nowhere. He approached the table and sat down. "You have something you wish to discuss with me?" he asked quietly.

"Indeed we do!" thundered Fergus.

"Calm down Fergus!" ordered Chief Fernlea in a forceful voice. "I will inform Kee of our findings."

He then dismissed Hamish and Misty before acquainting Kee with their report.

Granny was watching Hamish carefully. He had come in from his assignment quietly and now sat slouched on his stool at the fire, holding his head in his hands. Normally he returned from the Church and was full of stories about Jesus whom he appeared to have become quite fond of. She carried on chopping her vegetables watching him out of the corner of her eye and hoping he would break this silence and tell her what was troubling him. She had chopped enough cabbage to feed the whole clan and still Hamish had not moved or spoken. This was serious. This was not one of those times when he and Misty had fallen out. No, this was *serious*. She washed her hands, wiping them on her apron to dry them, before sitting down on her chair opposite Hamish in front of the fire.

"Are you going to tell me what has made you so upset?" she asked.

Slowly Hamish removed his hands from his face

and looked up at her. "Mistress MacLeod had died," Hamish sobbed. "I really liked her. She was a good, kind human and now she's gone."

Bit by bit, Hamish told his Granny all that had happened in the Church that morning. Granny listened intently. Mistress MacLeod had been a good human. She was sure the villagers would miss her. That Robert Kirk, on the other hand; how dare he tell their secrets! He had betrayed them all! He would have to pay the ultimate price.

"Hamish do you know what will happen to Robert Kirk now?" asked Granny.
"I think so," replied Hamish quietly.

Chapter 18

Robert Kirk was feeling good today. He had completed his service at the Church and nobody had wanted to stay for a chat afterwards so he was able to get home early. He had enjoyed a good roast beef dinner and was now on his way towards Doon Hill. As he approached the woods Kee suddenly appeared at his side.

"Good afternoon Kee. What a beautiful day don't you think?" Robert Kirk greeted him.
Kee made no reply but kept walking.
"My garden is blooming well, especially the roses," Robert continued.
Kee made no comment.
"I was thinking I would like to visit the Sylvan gardens today, please," Robert Kirk went on.
Kee still did not reply.
"Perhaps the elves would give me some of their seeds to plant in my own garden. What do you think?" Robert Kirk asked.

By now they had reached the entrance to the Knowe. Kee pushed aside the curtain, opened the door and beckoned Robert Kirk to enter.

As they walked down the tunnel, Kee finally answered Robert Kirk's question. "You won't be going to the gardens today; you will be meeting the King and Queen."

"Really?" replied Robert Kirk. "How super! I have not seen the King and Queen since my very first visit here. I hope they are both well."

Kee made no comment.

Inside the Royal chamber the King and Queen sat on their thrones as they had on his previous visit. Today, however, they were not smiling. Robert Kirk was at once aware of this and the hairs on the back of his neck stood to attention. The King stood up as Robert Kirk approached.

"You have betrayed us, Robert Kirk," stated the King.

"No.....no I don't think so," said Robert Kirk.

"Don't interrupt! You have told of our world to the humans in your Church," said the King coldly.

"I didn't mean to betray you. I just wanted the people to understand you better. I'm sorry if I have offended you," whimpered Robert Kirk.

"You told our secrets," repeated the King. "You were warned what would happen if you did this. We are going to keep you here, Robert Kirk!"

The King laid his hand on Robert Kirk's head. It felt cold. A cold wave crept down his neck and into his stomach before travelling down to his hands and feet. Robert felt as if his soul was being sucked out of him.

Margaret Kirk was worried. Her husband had gone out for a walk hours ago. He had never been this late home before. Several times she had walked to the end of the Manse's drive and looked up the track towards Doon Hill but nothing. She decided to go and look one final time. She put her coat on, and walked out once more. She reached the gate and looked up the track. It was empty. A sinking feeling began in the pit of her stomach. Looking in the opposite direction she saw their friend out walking his dog.

"John! John!" she shouted, running towards him. "Robert has not returned from his walk, hours ago. I think he must have had an accident!"
"Where did he go?" asked John McGregor.
"He went up Doon Hill as usual. I know something is wrong," Margaret replied.
"Go into the house. I'll go and fetch the doctor and some of the other men. We'll form a search party. Don't worry, we'll find him," said John.

Margaret returned to the house and put the kettle on. She was just finishing her third cup of tea when she heard footsteps and voices. Immediately she ran and opened the door. John stood before her with his bunnet in his hands. Behind him she could see several other men. Four of them were carrying a stretcher.

"I'm sorry, Margaret. Robert's dead," said John flatly.

She pushed past him and looked down at the figure lying on the stretcher. A huge sob stuck in her throat and she crumpled onto the ground.

"Let's get them both inside," John said.

The men left, except for John and Dr. McPherson. John made Margaret a strong cup of tea and sat her down in front of the fire.

"Where did you find him?" whispered Margaret.

"He was sitting, leaning against one of the trees, near the top of the hill. I thought he was asleep, at first," replied John.

"He must have sat down after the climb and his heart just gave out," said Dr McPherson quietly.

Margaret nodded in response.

"We've sent for the undertaker. He will bring a coffin for him and lay him out. The front room be alright?" asked Dr McPherson.

Again Margaret nodded.

Soon Archie Cameron arrived and laid Robert Kirk's body in the coffin. John led Margaret into her own front room. He placed an arm around her shoulder as she looked down at the face of her husband. Margaret noticed that Archie had dressed him in his best suit. She reached out and stroked Robert's cheek for the last time. As she did so a rumble of thunder rolled overhead, followed by a fork of lightning which lit up the whole room. Margaret trembled.

"Would you like some time alone with him?" asked Doctor McPherson.
Margaret shook her head. "Leave the lid off. People will want to come and pay their last respects," she said.

The two men then silently followed her back through to the kitchen. She sat down by the fire and poured herself another cup of tea.

"It's those dam Fair Folk!" Margaret suddenly shouted. "If he hadn't been so obsessed with them he would be here with me now."
The men looked at one another, unsure what to say at this outburst.
A knock at the door interrupted the silence.
"I'll get it," said John. "Someone to see the Minister, no doubt."
As he opened the door a voice yelled at him, "Come quickly! Bring the doctor! Lightning has struck the rowan trees beside Farmer Campbell's barn. With the wind blowing, it's on fire too!"
John turned back to Margaret. "I'm so sorry," he said. "We'll have to go and help."
Margaret waved her hand listlessly in recognition.

"Don't worry Margaret," said Doctor McPherson. "We will call back later."

When the men left Margaret hurled her half empty tea cup at the wall. As the tea dripped down the paint work, the tears spilled down Margaret's cheeks. She did not even attempt to dry them with her handkerchief.

She was unsure how long she sat there, but when she at last eased herself out of her chair, she noticed that the fire had burnt out and it was daylight. What a dreadful night! Had she been dreaming? She walked slowly from the kitchen to the front room. It hadn't been a dream. The evidence of that was staring at her. The coffin, supported by two coffin stools stood in the centre of the room. Margaret frowned. The lid had been put on. She was sure it had been open last night. A knock at the door brought her out of her thoughts.

"Good morning, Margaret," said John.
"Come in, John. Look at the coffin. Its lid is on," said Margaret.
"Did Archie Cameron come by earlier and do it?" asked John.
"No, you're the first here. I don't understand it," replied Margaret.
John crossed over to the coffin. "Would you like me to open it again?" he inquired.
"Yes please."

John found the lid was not sealed and he was able to simply lift it off and lay it down in the corner of the room. He stepped back to look at his friend one more time.

"Oh my God!" he exclaimed, suddenly turning very pale.
"What is wrong, John?" asked Margaret walking towards him.

Margaret looked from John's ashen face to the inside of the coffin and fainted at what she saw. Robert Kirk's body was no longer there. In its place was a heap of stones!

Chapter 19

Kee stood with his arms folded, gazing down on the body of Robert Kirk which was spread out on a stone slab in the centre of the "Waiting Cell". How could the face of this human look so calm, peaceful, innocent, when inside lay the black heart of betrayal? The door to this cell suddenly opened to reveal an elf standing on the threshold. Kee slowly lifted his head and looked at the elf.

"It is time," stated the elf, and left leaving the door ajar.

Kee knelt down over the body of Robert Kirk. He felt in his pocket and produced a small bottle. He took out the cork and left it hanging by a thread which was attached to the bottle's neck. With his right hand he opened Robert Kirk's mouth and poured the contents of the bottle between the parted lips. Then he re-corked the bottle, placed it back in his pocket, stood up and waited. He did not wait long. It took only minutes for the contents to do their job. Robert Kirk opened his eyes.

"It is time," stated Kee, "follow me."

Robert Kirk slid himself off the stone

slab, stood up shakily and proceeded to follow Kee from the cell out into a corridor, lit only by candles, until they reached a large cavern. Kirk remembered this cavern. He had been here twice before. As Kee stood aside, the King and Queen appeared, sitting on their thrones looking directly at him.

"Come forward, Robert Kirk," said the King.

Robert Kirk shuffled nervously towards them. He raised his head, straightened his shoulders and stood tall, ready to receive his punishment.

"You betrayed us, Robert Kirk," continued the King. "However, the Queen and I feel your betrayal was unintentional. You were hoping your human people would see us in a good way. Therefore instead of sending you directly to the quarries to work for us, we have decided to honour you with a chance to return to your world."

"Thank you," mumbled Robert Kirk. "I won't betray you again, I promise."

"We know that," replied the King. "You will go to your cousin with a message. You will tell him to go to your Laird, Graham of Duchray. His wife has just had a new baby. This baby will be baptised on Sunday. A party will then follow at your manse. You will make an appearance at this celebration. When Graham of Duchray sees you, he must throw a dagger over your head. This dagger must be made of iron as it is the only metal which can rescind the enchantment we have put upon you."

"I don't understand," stammered Robert Kirk. "Are you releasing me back to my world?"

"Your release is only temporary. If you do not follow these rules you will be brought straight back here without any chance of your freedom," explained the King.

"Can I not go and see my wife? She will be worried about me," asked Robert Kirk.

"Your wife thinks you are dead," announced the Queen who had been strangely quiet until now.

"Dead?" questioned Robert Kirk.

"Dead," answered the Queen, coldly.

"Do you understand your mission, Robert Kirk?" asked the King.

"I understand what I have to do but not why I have to do it," he replied.

"If you fail, you will remain here, working in our quarries – forever! There is nothing more for you to understand." answered the Queen.

"But....but..the Laird? Why the Laird?" asked Robert Kirk.

"You do not need to know," retorted the Queen.

"Take him away now, please Kee. There is nothing more we have to say here."

Kee led Robert Kirk out of the cavern, along the corridor and back into his cell.

"I will fetch you when the time comes for you to begin your mission," stated Kee before closing the door, leaving Robert Kirk alone with his thoughts.

As darkness fell in the human world, Kee was making his way back to the cell where Robert Kirk was imprisoned. He felt Robert Kirk was lucky to be given a chance to win back his freedom. The quarries already contained humans who had betrayed the Sidhe, some had been there for decades. Now it was up to Robert Kirk himself to persuade his cousin he was for real and to take the message to the Laird. Robert Kirk's life was now in the hands of Graham of Duchray.

Chapter 20

Mac was confused. He was getting ready to go the baptism of the Laird's baby, yet he could not get his cousin, Robert Kirk, out of his mind. Robert had filled his thoughts for almost a week now. Firstly he had been found dead up on Doon Hill and taken back to the Manse. Then his body had disappeared, only to be replaced by a pile of stones. Then three nights ago he had appeared to him in a dream. Only it didn't feel like a dream. It felt real, as if Robert was there, talking to him at his bedside in the middle of the night. He had a message for him to pass onto the Laird. He still had not said a word to the Laird about it but it had dogged him continuously. What if he said nothing and Robert did appear at the baptism? What if he did say to the Laird and nothing happened? What a dilemma! He continued his struggle with his collar stud.

"Will you please hurry up or we will be late," his wife's voice intruded into his thoughts.
"Just coming," he answered as he rushed down the stairs and into the hallway where his wife was waiting for him.

The baptism went without any hitches. As Robert Kirk's deputy gently poured the holy water over the child's forehead Mac still struggled with his dilemma. Time was running out! What should he do?

It was only a ten minute walk from the church to the Manse. Mac decided it was now or never. He skirted past some of the other guests until he reached the Laird. He excused himself and begged Graham of Duchray to listen to his story. Needless to say the Laird was awestruck but promised to fulfil the task if indeed Robert did put in an appearance. Mac felt strangely lightened as he dropped back amongst the crowd and was rejoined by his wife.

The celebration was in full swing. The company had just eaten a delicious roast beef dinner followed by dumpling covered in creamy custard. Mac sat back in his chair; full up with good food and relaxed for the first time in days. He had unburdened himself to the Laird who did not laugh at him but treated him fairly. Robert had not appeared. It *had* been a dream. Obviously the shock of Robert's death had been playing with his sub-conscious. He smiled to himself. How silly he had been to even consider the fact that Robert would appear before them when he was dead!

The Laird stood up and smiled round at his guests. "I would just like to thank you for coming today and joining my wife and I, in the celebration of our child's baptism. It was extremely kind of Margaret to allow us to gather here at the Manse so soon after Robert's passing. Pass round the whisky and fill your glasses. I would like to propose a toast to......"

The Laird halted in mid-stream. He appeared frozen, as if suddenly turned to stone. He stared at the open door. A sudden coldness entered the room making his guests shiver. Their eyes were drawn to the doorway. There, dressed in his minister's full regalia, stood Robert Kirk. He stared at Graham of Duchray, pleading to him with his eyes to do something. The sunlight caught the glass in his out stretched hand, sending rainbows circling around the company. An eerie silence filled the room. No one moved. No one spoke. *No one did anything!* The dancing rainbows began gathering around Robert Kirk until he was completely surrounded by them. The sun disappeared behind a cloud, thus killing the rainbows........... and Robert Kirk! As the sun returned to fill the room with its light; the doorway was empty!

The King and Queen of the Sidhe sat grandly on their thrones. They looked down on all their tribes which had gathered in the cavern. They had been called to witness the demise of Robert Kirk – minister of the church, intruder of Doon Hill, betrayer of the Sidhe!

In the centre of the throng two gnomes stood side by side waiting…….

"Do you think he will come back?" asked Hamish.
"I don't know. It could go either way," answered Misty.
"I think he was jolly lucky to be given another chance," said Hamish.
"Ssh, something is about to happen. I feel it in the air," Misty replied.

The bright light in the cavern dimmed to be replaced by many colours swirling round and round over the heads of the gnomes and other tribes. The King stood up and raised his right hand as a signal to the lights to collect and come before him. They descended quickly and on reaching the floor, took up the form of elves. They drew slightly back causing the rest of the assembly to take a few steps backwards too. A solitary figure was left standing before the Royals.

"You have returned to us, Robert Kirk," declared the King.
Robert Kirk nodded.
The Queen rose to her feet and pointed at Robert Kirk. "You will remain with us now: forever!"
The King snapped his fingers and Kee appeared beside the dejected figure of Robert Kirk. "Take him to the quarries!"

As Kee led Robert Kirk through the throng, a buzz of whispering broke out. Everyone seemed to have an opinion on what was happening.

"Well," said Hamish. "I guess the humans were too scared when he appeared before them."

"Maybe," answered Misty. "What ever happened he will now work in the quarries as his punishment and we won't be seeing him again."

"It will be so good to get back to normal duties once more. Don't you think so?" enquired Hamish.

"Yes, it will be," agreed Misty.

"It will soon be the longest day, with the biggest party and loads of food and dancing and singing............and I just can't wait!" declared Hamish.

Chapter 21

Hamish was sitting on the fallen log that was also his look out post. He was not looking for intruders but passing his time whittling away on a piece of wood. Every now and then he cast his eyes skywards, taking in the path of the setting sun and calculating the time of daylight he had left before the sun went to sleep. Now it was Autumn, the sun and moon shared the day equally. Hamish liked Autumn. He liked the vibrant colours that nature wore before winter took over and covered every thing in grey. He liked the way all the creatures began to cosy down for winter, some for the long sleep until spring, others to wake periodically. He liked the way his tribe and humans gathered in their harvests to feed themselves through out the coming cold times. Most of all, he liked the harvest celebration party.

Hamish thought back to the last party he had enjoyed. It was in Summer, not long after Robert Kirk had paid the penalty for his betrayal. He did not feel sorry for Kirk at all. After all, he had been warned what would happen should he disclose anything he had seen. He had even been given a second chance, but the humans had not fulfilled the necessary conditions that would have granted him his freedom. All said and done, Hamish was quite relieved that this particular chapter in Sidhe history had been closed.

"What are **you** doing, sitting there day dreaming when we have a party to go to?" Misty's question interrupted his thoughts.

"Just passing the time," answered Hamish, hastily shoving his knife and the piece of wood into his pockets.

"Show me!" demanded Misty, stretching her hand out towards him.

"Show you what?" asked Hamish sheepishly.

"Whatever it was that you just shoved into your pockets," Misty retorted.

"I don't know what you mean," began Hamish.

"Just show me!"

Hamish knew he would get no peace until he did so. He pushed his hand into his pocket and produced the effort of his labours.

"It's beautiful," gasped Misty, stroking the piece of wood. "You've carved a beautiful hen out of an old piece of branch."

"Thank you."

"Why did you choose a hen?" she inquired.

"Please don't laugh," sighed Hamish. "I made it for Mistress MacLeod. She always wanted a hen didn't she?"

"That's a lovely thought, Hamish," answered Misty quietly, "but she's dead, you remember?"

"I know she's dead. I'm not a fool. I knew you would laugh at me!"

"I'm not laughing, Hamish," continued Misty gently. "I just don't know what you are going to do with it."

"Tomorrow night when we are on patrol, I'm going down to her grave and bury it in there," Hamish stated defiantly.

"You're really quite kind and thoughtful, aren't you Hamish. Would you mind if I tagged along too?" Misty asked.

"No, as long as you don't think I'm daft!"

"No I don't think that. Put it away safely, perhaps in your inside pocket of your tunic. You don't want to lose it do you?"

Hamish nodded in agreement, and still looking at Misty, he shoved the wooden hen down deep into his inside pocket.

"Ouch!" he screamed, withdrawing his hand quickly.

"What have you done?" asked Misty, noticing one of his fingers was bleeding.

"I forgot that my arrows are in there, didn't I?"

"I thought you'd used them all up!" said Misty.

"I had. I went back to collect them afterwards, but I could only find two of them. I decided to keep them with me should we need them again," mumbled Hamish as he attempted to speak and suck his bleeding finger at the same time.

"Anyway, is it not time we were getting along to this party? I don't want all the food to go before I get there,"

As they rose to their feet, the first glimpse of the pale harvest moon was appearing in the east. Shortly its colour would deepen and light up the woods almost as well as the sun had during the day. They had not walked very far though, when they came upon a strange sight. A robin was scraping about on the forest floor with its feet, while clutching something in its beak!

"What are you doing out here at this time of the evening? Don't you ever sleep?" inquired Misty.

The robin kept scraping away but did not answer.

"Should you not be settling down in your roost?" asked Hamish.

The robin continued with its task paying no heed to the gnomes.

"Can we help you to do whatever it is you are trying to do?" persisted Misty.

The robin spat on the ground dislodging whatever it was in its beak.

"I am trying to help you!" she replied.

Hamish and Misty both recognised this robin now. She was the special robin who kept popping up just when they needed her.

"What are you doing?" asked Hamish, kneeling down beside her and retrieving whatever she had had in her break. He looked at it carefully.

"It's a seed from a pine cone. They don't grow in this wood. Why do you have it?"

"I flew away to the pine forests and brought it back here to plant it," she answered.

"Why?" asked Misty curiously.

"When this seed grows, it will obviously grow into a pine tree," began the robin. "As you say it will be different to any others in this wood. I hope when you see it, it will remind you that it doesn't belong here. It will remind you that you should not entertain creatures here that don't belong."

"I don't understand what you mean," replied Hamish.

"Humans! Robert Kirk! They don't belong; just like this tree," stated the exasperated robin.

"I get it," shouted Misty. "It's to remind us not to invite humans into our world."

"That's right," replied the robin, "now go to your party and let me finish my work so I can go to my roost."

The harvest moon, now bright orange in colour, shone down on Doon Hill. Gnomes were appearing from their underground homes into its light. Chief Fernlea led the way to the Knowe. He was followed by Fergus, David, Donald, Torquil and McBeth. Hamish and Misty hurried to join the throng. They were greeted by Granny and Calum and all walked along together. As far as the gnomes were concerned there was nothing better than a party!

Not far from the hill, someone else was

watching the harvest moon's progress from the east. She did not feel the excitement of the gnomes. Her heart felt cold and heavy. She stared at the moon wistfully.

"Oh Robert, why did you have to go and leave me? Why did you need to find out about the Sidhe?" Margaret Kirk uttered.

Eventually Margaret turned from the window. She looked at the room Robert had called his study. She was leaving the Manse in a few days. A new minister would be taking Robert's place. Only the top drawer of his desk was left to be emptied. Robert had never let anyone into this drawer, in fact he had kept it locked at all times. Margaret, cautiously placed the key in the lock, turned it and opened the drawer. Many sheaves of paper met her eyes. She wasn't really sure what she'd expected to find there, something valuable or secret perhaps but instead, just a load of papers! She lifted the topmost ones out and flicked through them. Writing, in Robert's own hand, paintings of strange beings. What was this? Her eyes were drawn to one page, the only words written there were *'The Secret Lives of Elves and Faeries!'*

Furiously, she threw the papers into the open trunk beside the desk. She delved into the drawer again, bringing out the remainder of the pile. Something dropped from them and fell onto the floor beside her foot. She dumped the sheets into the trunk with the others. Bending down to examine what had fallen, she saw a slim piece of tapering wood with green feathers sticking out of one end. She stretched her hand out and carefully picked it up. It looked suspiciously like a small dart or arrow. She turned and threw it into the trunk to join the papers. She kicked the lid down with as much force as she could. Tears streaming down her face, she strode to the window, opened it wide and leaned out. Shaking her fist in the direction of Doon Hill, she yelled,

"Dam you faery folk! You've stolen my husband!"

Glossary

Bunnet.................................Flat cap

Chanty.................................Chamber pot

Coup....................................Rubbish dump

Dyke.....................................Wall

Girdle...................................A circular plate of iron used for cooking on.

Jammy Piece.......................Jam Sandwich

Kin.......................................Family

Press....................................Cupboard or closet

Skelp....................................Slap or smack

Spirtle..................................A wooden stick for stirring porridge

About the Author

Janette Bond was born and brought up in Aberfoyle, a small village in Central Scotland. She worked there as a primary school teacher for 26 years. She has a great interest in the local history of The Trossachs area. She also has a great passion for literature. Combining both of these attributes with her knowledge of what children like to read and listen to, she has written this novel to bring alive one of the best known legends of this area.

Lightning Source UK Ltd.
Milton Keynes UK
13 March 2011

169159UK00001B/21/P